For Glenis Redmond, who knows where she is
AW

To Mark Sperring
LT

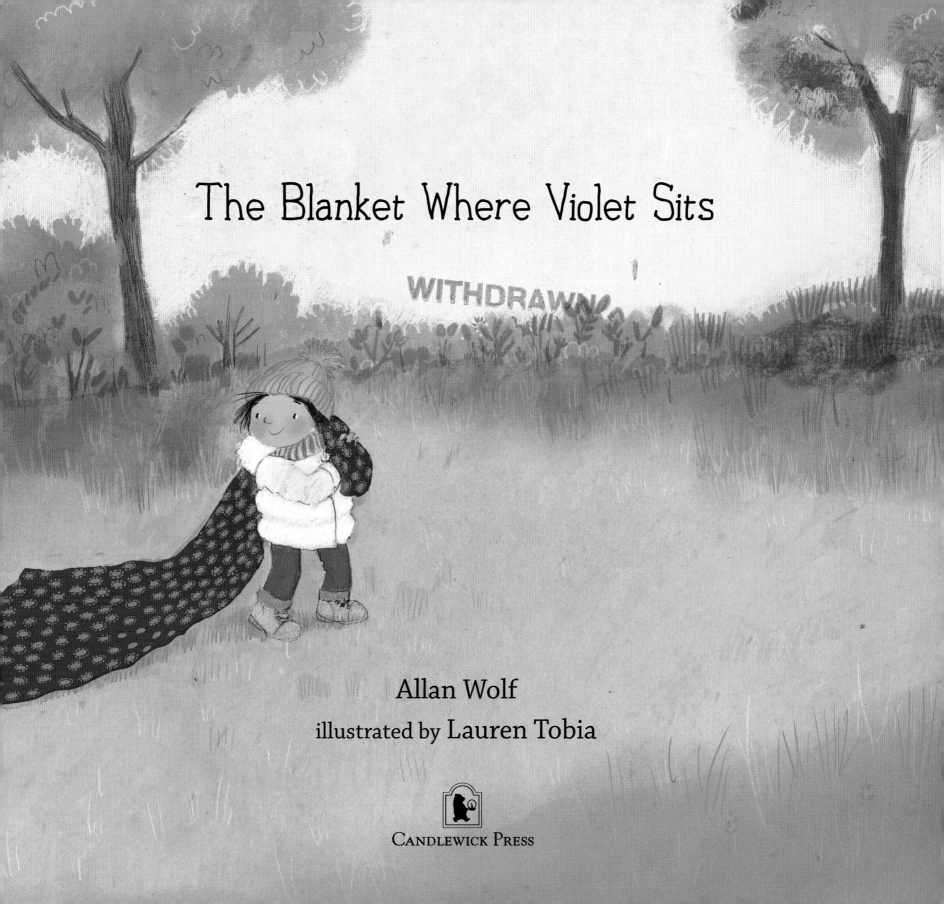

The Blanket Where Violet Sits

Allan Wolf

illustrated by Lauren Tobia

CANDLEWICK PRESS

THIS IS THE BLANKET where Violet sits,
eating a sandwich, an apple, and chips.

This is the park in the bustling city,
home to the blanket where Violet sits,
eating a sandwich, an apple, and chips.

This is the planet with a moon so pretty
that shines on the park in the bustling city,
home to the blanket where Violet sits,
eating a sandwich, an apple, and chips.

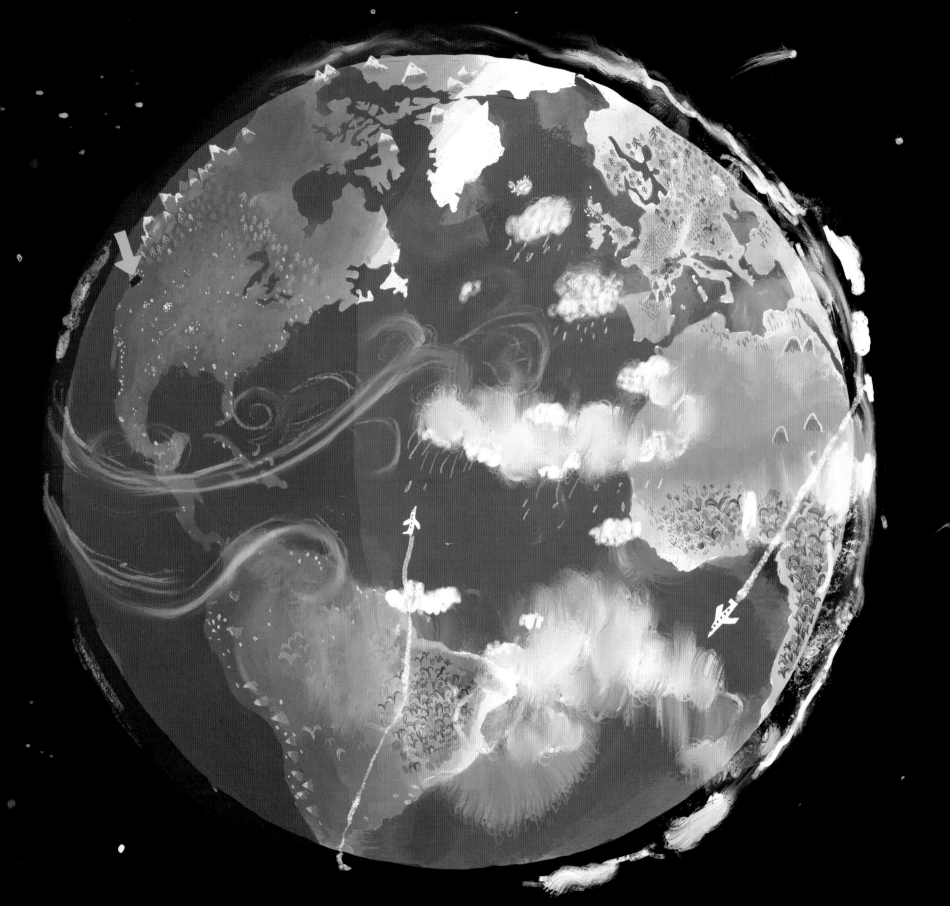

This is the yellow star, orbited 'round

by the small blue planet with a moon so pretty
that shines on the park in the bustling city,
home to the blanket where Violet sits,
eating a sandwich, an apple, and chips.

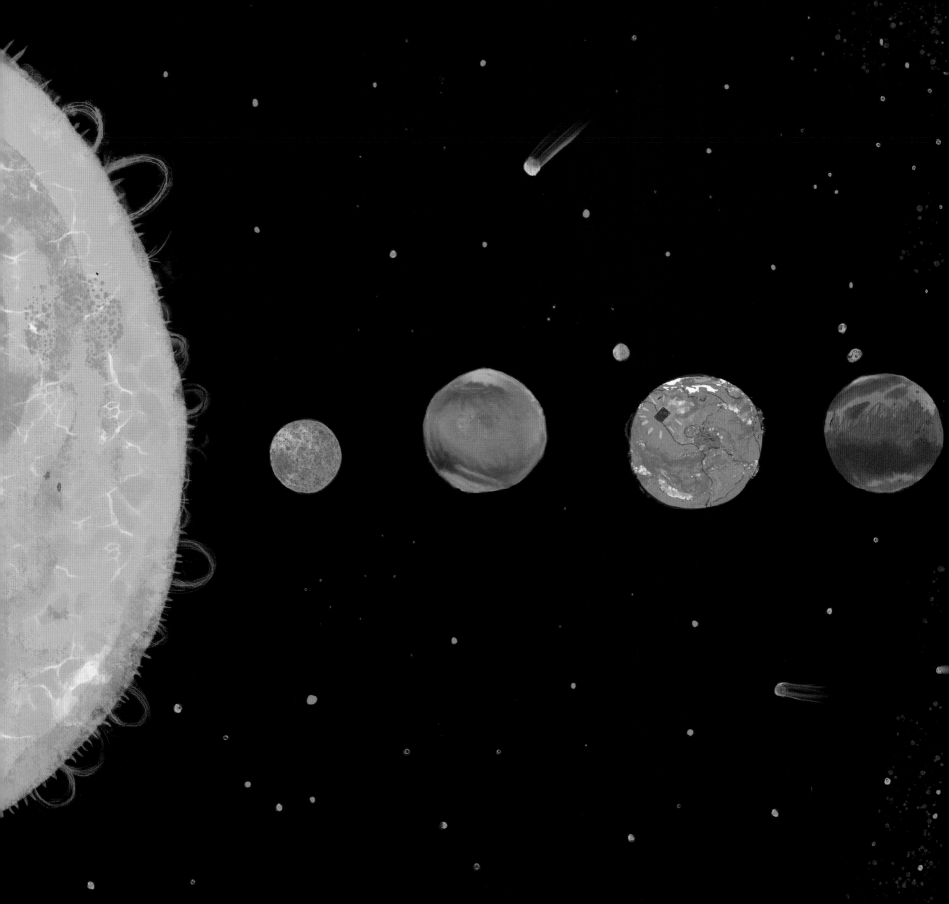

This is the solar system whose eight planets surround
the warm yellow star that is orbited 'round

by the tiny blue planet with a moon so pretty

that shines on the park in the bustling city,

home to the blanket where Violet sits,

eating a sandwich, an apple, and chips.

This is the galaxy, spiraling white.
And here on this spot, if you look just right,
is the solar system whose eight planets surround

the warm yellow star that is orbited 'round
by the tiny blue planet with a moon so pretty
that shines on the park in the bustling city,
home to the blanket where Violet sits,
eating a sandwich, an apple, and chips.

Here are two thousand galaxies clustered in clouds,

home to one galaxy spiraling white,

where on this spot, if you look just right,

is the solar system where eight planets surround

the warm yellow star that is orbited 'round

by the tiny blue planet with a moon so pretty

that shines on the park in the bustling city,

home to the blanket where Violet sits,

eating a sandwich, an apple, and chips.

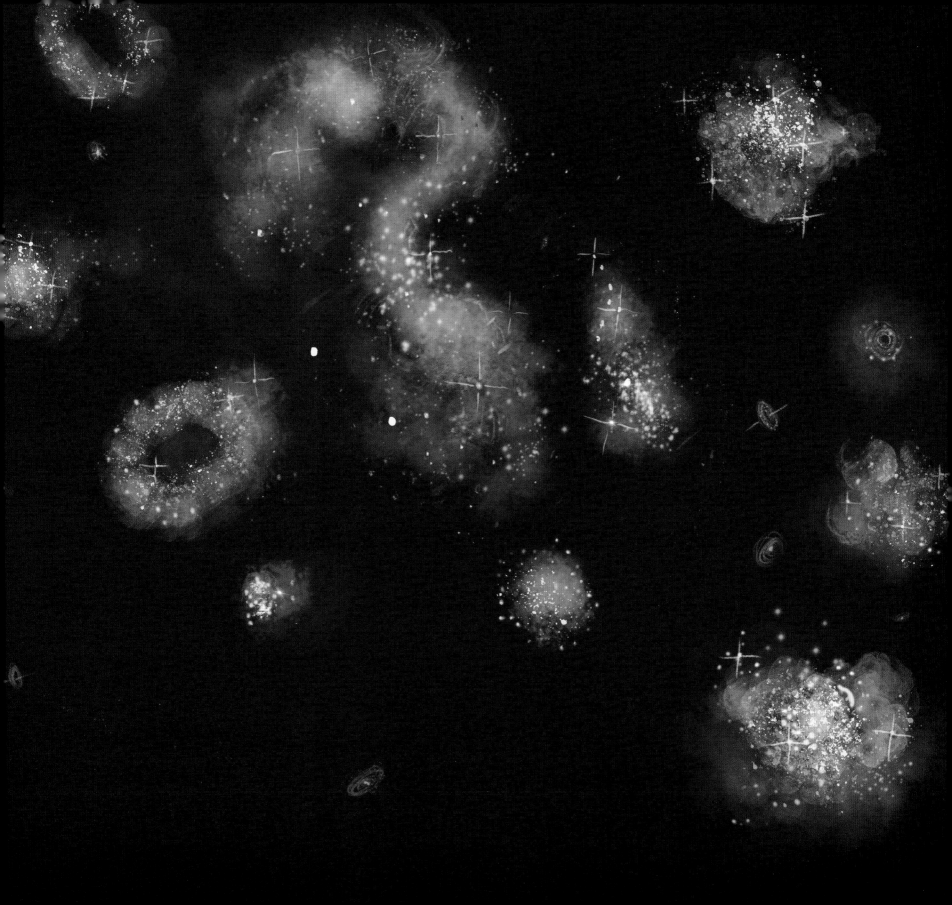

Here's the known universe, past comprehension,
billions of light-years in every direction
and billions of galaxies out in the black.

There might be a Violet out there, looking back
at our own little galaxy spiraling white,
where on this spot here, if you look just right,

is our own solar system where eight planets surround
a warm yellow star that is orbited 'round

by a jewel-blue planet with a moon so pretty
that shines on the park in the bustling city,

home to the blanket where Violet sits,
done with her sandwich, her apple, and chips.